TWELVE SHORT MYSTERY,

Adventure and other stories

With a moral and a twist

(and maybe a few jokes)

FOR AGES 8-15

Paul Hill

Dedication

For Amelie and Laurence

And all those who have encouraged me including:

Jo, Barbie, Alan, Jane, Brittany, Chris,

Alan, Daniel, Ryan, Dean, Simon

and Theo

CHOOSE A STORY!

The Clown who ran away from the Circus

A Carshalton Haunting

Detective Sterling and the Railway Mystery

Simon Schutte and the Pioneers of Space

The New School

The Monkey and the Elephant

Shadowfang

Detective Alex AI

Queen of Gridiron

Jack and Mary. A story from the first World War

Whodunnit?

Two bonus stories – for those who can't wait for the next book!

Theo, Amelie, and the Doll's House

Racing to the Maxx

THE CLOWN WHO RAN AWAY FROM THE CIRCUS

Once upon a time, in a land far, far away, there lived a clown named Joe. He had been a part of the circus for as long as he could remember, entertaining audiences with his silly antics and goofy jokes. He loved the thrill of performing in front of a crowd, and the sound of their laughter was music to his ears. However, deep down, Joe was not content with his life.

Joe worked in a traditional circus, filled with all the classic elements one would expect. There was a big tent that served as the main stage, where acrobats, clowns, and other performers would put on shows for the audience. The smell of sawdust, popcorn, and cotton candy filled the air, creating a festive atmosphere.

The circus was home to a diverse cast of performers, each with their own unique talents. There were tightrope walkers, jugglers, and animal trainers, who would dazzle the crowds with their skills. The clowns were the heart and soul of the circus, bringing laughter and joy to the audience with their silly jokes and antics.

The ringmaster, a charismatic individual, would introduce each act with flair and panache, keeping the audience engaged and entertained. The circus was a traveling show, moving from town to town, setting up in a new location each week. The performers lived in colourful trailers and caravans that were parked on the outskirts of each town, forming a tight-knit community.

Despite the hard work and long hours, the circus was a place of magic and wonder, and Joe was proud to be a part of it. However, as he grew older, he began to yearn for something more, and that's when he decided to run away.

He didn't like the long hours and the constant travel, never staying in one place for long. He missed his family and friends and yearned for a normal life. The circus had become a cage for him, a prison that he couldn't escape from. He felt trapped, and the once joyous feelings of performing had turned into a chore.

One night, while the circus was in town, Joe decided that he couldn't take it anymore. He packed his bags and left in the middle of the night, not telling anyone where he was going or why. He just wanted to be free, to live his life on his own terms.

As Joe walked down the road, he felt a weight lifted off of his shoulders. He realized that he had been living in a cage for so long and now he was finally free. The fresh air, the sound of nature, and the freedom to go wherever he wanted was a feeling he had never experienced before. He felt alive, and the future looked bright.

But as the days went on, Joe began to feel lonely. He missed the camaraderie of the circus and the feeling of making people happy. He realized that even though he had escaped the physical cage of the circus, he was still trapped in the cage of his own mind. He missed the joy of performing and making people laugh, but he was determined to find a new way to do it.

Joe decided to use his talents to make people laugh in his own way. He started performing in small towns and villages, putting on shows for anyone who would watch. He found that he enjoyed this new way of life even more than being in the circus. He was able to travel to new places and meet new people, all while doing what he loved. He was free to create his own schedule and perform on his own terms.

Years went by and Joe became known as the "clown who ran away from the circus." He was happy and fulfilled, and he never looked back. However, just when he thought he had found his true calling in life and was grateful for the opportunity to be free, he received a letter from the circus. It turns out that the circus was in dire straits and was about to close down. The ringmaster, who was a dear friend of Joe, pleaded with him to come back and save the circus.

Joe was torn, he didn't want to go back to the circus, but he couldn't bear the thought of his beloved circus closing down. He decided to go back, and with his help, the circus was able to turn things around and became more successful than ever before. Joe was able to perform again and make people happy, but this time, he was doing it on his own terms, and he was finally truly free. He had found a way to combine his love of performing with his need for freedom and lived happily ever after.

CLOWN JOKES

Did you hear about the clown who ran away with the circus? They made him bring it back.

A friend of mine is an expert in making clown shoes. It's no small feat.

Another friend has just got a steady job. He's a tightrope walker in a circus.

What material is a clown's costume made from? Poly Jester.

I had a friend who was a clown who performed on stilts. I always looked up to him.

Saw a group of pheasants & partridges dressed as clowns. I thought, "they're game for a laugh".

A friend worked as a trapeze artist until he was let go.

A CARSHALTON HAUNTING

Two adventurous siblings, Emily and Jack, lived in the small town of Carshalton. They were always on the lookout for new and exciting experiences, so when they heard rumours about a haunted house on the outskirts of town, they couldn't resist checking it out.

As they approached the house, they noticed that it was situated on a sprawling property and appeared to be abandoned for many years. Despite the creepy appearance of the house, the siblings were eager to explore the interior.

Upon entering the house, they were immediately struck by the eerie silence that pervaded the air. It felt as though they had stepped into a different world, one that was haunted by the ghosts of its past residents. They looked around in wonder, taking in the dusty furniture, cobweb-covered chandeliers, and eerie portraits hanging on the walls.

Suddenly, they heard a creaking sound coming from upstairs. Emily and Jack cautiously climbed the stairs, their nerves on edge as they anticipated what they might find. They were amazed when they reached the top of the stairs and found themselves in a dark room. In the centre of the room stood a mysterious figure shrouded in shadows.

The figure stepped forward, revealing itself to be a ghostly woman with long, flowing hair and glowing eyes. At first, the siblings were terrified, but then they noticed the mischievous twinkle in her eye. The ghostly woman chuckled and explained that she was the resident prankster ghost of the haunted house.

"I've been scaring people in this house for years," she said with a wicked grin. "And it's about time I had some company."

Emily and Jack, who had come to the haunted house expecting to find a frightening experience, were instead delighted to discover that they had found a friend in the form of the prankster ghost. The ghostly woman was full of energy and fun, and she showed the siblings all sorts of hidden rooms and secret passages throughout the house.

As they explored the haunted house, they encountered several other ghosts, each with their own personalities and quirks. There was the grumpy ghost who lived in the basement, the mischievous ghost who liked to play tricks on visitors, and the friendly ghost who loved to tell stories.

The siblings and the ghostly residents of the haunted house spent the rest of the day playing pranks on each other, making ghostly noises, and exploring the haunted house. Emily and Jack were having the time of their lives, and the ghostly residents of the house were overjoyed to have someone to share their mischief with.

As the sun began to set, the siblings reluctantly made their way back home. They were filled with excitement and laughter, and they couldn't wait to return to the haunted house and their new friends, the ghostly residents of the house.

From that day on, the haunted house was no longer a place of fear and mystery, but instead, it was a place of laughter and fun. The people of Carshalton were amazed at the transformation, but only Emily and Jack knew the real reason behind the change: the power of friendship and the joy of playing pranks together with the ghostly residents of the haunted house.

GHOST JOKES

What do you call a ghost detective? An inspectre

What did the Ghost Teacher say to the class? Keep your eyes on the board whilst I go through it again

What is a Ghosts favourite dessert? I-Scream!

What room doesn't a Ghost need in his house? A living room!

Where do fancy Ghosts go shopping? A boo-tique!

How does a Ghost unlock a door? Using a Spoo-Key!

How did the Ghost get from New York to London? British Scare-ways!

Why didn't the Ghost go to the school prom? It has no-body to go with!

DETECTIVE STERLING AND THE RAILWAY MYSTERY

In the late 19th century, a string of mysterious disappearances rocked the bustling railway town of Coalville. Passengers on board various steam locomotives were disappearing without a trace.

Detective James Sterling was called in to investigate. He was a seasoned detective, with years of experience solving complex cases. But this one was different. The disappearances seemed to have no pattern or motive.

Detective James Sterling was a man of mystery, even to those who knew him best. He was a man of few words, but his reputation as a brilliant detective spoke for itself. He had a keen mind and a talent for solving complex cases that had stumped other detectives.

Growing up, James had always been fascinated by the workings of the mind. He studied psychology and criminology at university, and after graduation, he joined the police force. His natural talent for detective work soon became apparent, and he quickly rose through the ranks.

In his years on the force, James had solved many high-profile cases, but the case of the disappearing passengers on the steam locomotives of Coalville was unlike anything he had ever encountered. It was a challenge that he relished, and he threw himself into the investigation with his usual determination and tenacity.

As he delved deeper into the case, he learned about the different types of locomotives that plied the railways. There were the powerful and fast Express locomotives, the reliable and sturdy Freight locomotives, and the small and nimble Tank locomotives. Each had their own strengths and weaknesses, and each was capable of carrying passengers.

Despite his success, James was a deeply private man.

He lived alone in a small apartment, and few knew anything about his personal life. He was a solitary figure, but those who worked with him respected him for his intelligence and his unwavering commitment to justice.

And so, when the people of Coalville called upon Detective James Sterling to solve the mystery of the disappearing passengers, they knew that they were in good hands. And he did not disappoint.

Detective James Sterling's methodical and tenacious approach to the case was key to solving the mystery of the disappearing passengers on the steam locomotives. He began by interviewing witnesses and examining the evidence, but as the case progressed, he realized that the solution was not going to be found through traditional detective work.

He remembered a lecture he had attended on the subject of railway mechanics, and he had a sudden realization. The culprit must be someone with a deep understanding of steam locomotives and the power they wielded. And with that realization, the pieces began to fall into place.

He started to investigate the employees of the railway company, looking for anyone who had a passion for steam locomotives. And that's when he discovered the chief engineer, a brilliant inventor and mechanic who had become obsessed with the trains.

Detective Sterling arranged for a test ride on one of the trains, hoping to lure the culprit into action. And it worked. In the middle of the night, the lights went out, and Detective Sterling heard a scuffle in the next compartment. He cautiously approached, only to find the conductor lying unconscious on the floor. And the passenger in the compartment was nowhere to be found.

With this evidence, Detective Sterling had all he needed to make an arrest. He and the local authorities quickly apprehended the chief engineer, who was found to be the mastermind behind the disappearances.

The trial was a sensation, and the people of Coalville were shocked to learn that the brilliant and trusted chief engineer was the culprit. But Detective Sterling's unwavering commitment to justice and his determination to solve the case had brought the culprit to justice and put an end to the mystery of the disappearing passengers.

DETECTIVE JOKES

Why do detectives have such bad posture?

Because they always have a hunch.

How did the detective figure out who the engineer murdered?

He found his locomotive.

Yesterday, someone stole every single toilet from the local police station.

Today, detectives still have nothing to go on.

Detective one "I think the accountant did it, I found a calculator at the crime scene"

Detective two "That adds up"!

What do you call an estate agency opened by a detective?

Sherlock-homes!

What do you call a detective who solves cases accidentally?

Sheer-luck Holmes!

Did you hear about the detective who dropped his phone?

He cracked the case!

SIMON SCHUTTE AND THE PIONEERS OF SPACE

In the late 21st century, humanity had made remarkable advancements in space travel. With the discovery of Element-X, a powerful new source of energy, countries around the world formed the International Space Exploration Agency (ISE) to explore and colonize new worlds.

Simon was a young and ambitious astronaut, who grew up with a passion for space exploration. His dream was to be part of the elite crew that would embark on a journey to uncharted territories. When he was selected for the mission to explore a distant planet, he felt like his dream was finally becoming a reality.

The rest of the team consisted of six members: Dr. Maya Patel, a scientist specializing in geology, Dr. David Kim, a scientist specializing in planetary atmospheres, Dr. Elena Rodriguez, a scientist specializing in biochemistry, Mark Jenkins, an engineer and Linda Chen, an engineer.

They spent months training for the mission, and when the day finally arrived, they were ready for anything that the unknown might bring.

As they travelled further from Earth, the team encountered strange readings and malfunctions in their ship's systems. Despite their best efforts, they couldn't pinpoint the source of the problems and their mission was in jeopardy.

One day, as they approached the planet, their ship was suddenly struck by a massive burst of energy, causing all their systems to shut down. After their ship was struck by the burst of energy, the team was forced to abandon ship and make an emergency landing on the planet. They found that the energy burst had caused significant damage to the ship's systems, and they were unable to power it up again. With no other options, the team was forced to abandon ship and make an emergency landing on the surface of the planet.

As they stepped out of their ship, they were met with a world unlike any they had ever seen. The planet was inhospitable, with dangerous creatures and harsh environmental conditions that threatened their survival. Despite this, they were determined to complete their mission and collect samples of Element-X.

The team split up, with Simon leading one group and Mark and Linda heading another. As they ventured further into the unknown, they encountered many challenges and obstacles, but their resolve was unwavering. They relied on their training, ingenuity, and teamwork to overcome these difficulties.

During their mission, the team encountered strange and unknown creatures on the planet. One of these creatures was a formidable and dangerous alien. their mission took a dangerous turn when Elena was attacked by the creature.

The alien was a truly unique and awe-inspiring being, unlike anything they had ever seen before. It was a towering, organic creature, with a powerful build and a smooth, ethereal skin that glowed with a soft, iridescent light.

Its body was covered in shimmering, iridescent

feathers, and its eyes were large, black pools that seemed to reflect the very essence of the universe. The alien moved with grace and fluidity, its movements almost seeming to flow like water.

Despite its peaceful appearance, the alien was fiercely territorial and did not take kindly to the team's presence on its planet. When the team encountered it, the alien let out a powerful, ear-piercing screech, and charged at them with lightning speed.

Despite the danger, Simon and his team stood their ground and used their wits and training to fend off the alien. They eventually managed to communicate with it, and learned that the alien was simply trying to protect its home and family from perceived threats.

This encounter with the alien was a defining moment for the team, and they learned the importance of respecting other life forms and cultures, even in the unknown reaches of space. They had faced a formidable opponent and had come to understand it, and their bravery and determination had once again inspired future generations of space explorers.

Simon and his team continued their mission, and eventually they succeeded in collecting the samples they needed. Despite the challenges, Simon and his team were not ready to give up. They had brought with them limited resources and tools, and they knew they had to use their expertise and knowledge to repair the ship.

The engineers, Mark and Linda, assessed the damage to the ship's systems and found that several critical components had been damaged beyond repair. They came up with a plan to scavenge for materials on the planet to replace the damaged parts.

Dr. David and Dr. Maya helped the engineers by analysing the planet's atmosphere and geology, respectively, to find resources that could be used for the repairs.

With their combined knowledge and expertise, Mark and Linda and his team were able to fix the ship's systems and make it space-worthy again. They tested the ship's engines and, after several attempts, managed to take off from the planet and make their way back to Earth.

This was a major triumph for the team, and their ingenuity and determination in the face of adversity was a testament to the human spirit. They had overcome significant challenges and had completed their mission, despite the many dangers and obstacles they had faced along the way.

Upon their return, they were greeted as heroes and their bravery and determination inspired future generations of space explorers. Simon and his team had faced danger, uncertainty and unexpected challenges, but they had persevered, and their mission would forever be remembered as a defining moment in the history of space exploration.

This story is a testament to the human spirit, and a reminder of the dangers and uncertainties that come with venturing into the unknown. The pioneers of space flight showed that anything is possible with determination and the courage to face adversity head-on.

SPACE JOKES

What was the first animal in space? The cow that jumped over the moon!

What did Mars say to Saturn? Give me a ring sometime

Learning about space all day is exhausting. I need a launch break.

Orion's Belt is a huge waist of space.

I want to be an astronaut when I grow up but my mum says I have high hopes.

Astronauts are the only people who keep their jobs after they get fired

A pair of twins decided on adventurous careers.

One became an astronaut. The other became a skydiver. He was more down to earth.

THE NEW SCHOOL

Once upon a time, there was a young schoolgirl named Sally. She was known for being feisty and determined, but she had one fear: changing schools.

Sally was a determined and ambitious young girl, with a passion for learning and a strong sense of justice. She was not afraid to speak her mind and stand up for what she believed in, and her classmates admired her for her courage and conviction. She was a natural leader, and her classmates often looked to her for guidance and support.

Sally had always attended the same school, but her family was moving to a new town, and she would have to start at a new school in the middle of the year. She was nervous about making new friends and fitting in with the other students.

Despite her fear, Sally put on a brave face and headed off to her first day of school. As she walked through the halls, she felt the stares of the other students, and her nerves began to get the best of her. But just as she was about to retreat to the safety of her old school, she heard a friendly voice calling her name.

It was a girl named Jane, who had also recently moved to the town. She had noticed Sally's nervousness and offered to show her around the school.

Jane, was a more easy-going and outgoing person. She was friendly and approachable, and always had a smile on her face. She was also very empathetic and had a talent for making others feel at ease. She was a great listener and always had a kind word of encouragement for her friends. Together, Sally and Jane made a great team, balancing each other out and bringing out the best in one another.

At first, Sally was a bit hesitant to make friends with Jane, since she was not sure if they will get along. But as soon as they start talking, Sally realized that Jane was the kind of person she needed in her new school. Jane helped Sally to ease into the new school and feel more comfortable with the new environment and the new people. They started hanging out together, during lunch and after school, and quickly became close friends.

From that day forward, Sally and Jane were

inseparable. They helped each other navigate the new school and made many new friends along the way. Sally's confidence grew, and she became a well-respected and beloved member of the school community.

Sally's grades improved, and she started participating in extracurricular activities, like the debate team and student council. Jane was always there to support her and cheer her on. They were both happy to have found a friend who understood and accepted them for who they were.

Sally realized that sometimes the things we fear the most can turn out to be the best things that ever happen to us. She was grateful for her new school and the friends she had made, and she knew that she would always look back on her first day with fondness.

As time passed, Sally and Jane's friendship continued to grow stronger. They were inseparable, and their classmates knew that they were the best of friends. But just as Sally was beginning to feel truly settled in her new school, a twist in the story occurred.

It was revealed that Jane was moving away. Her family was relocating to a different area, and she would have to leave the school and her friends behind. Sally was devastated. She couldn't imagine going back to feeling alone and lost without her best friend by her side.

Sally and Jane made the most of the time they had left together, and they promised to stay in touch and visit each other whenever they could. But even with their promises, Sally knew that things would never be the same without Jane.

On the day of Jane's departure, Sally felt like her heart was breaking. She hugged her best friend tightly, not wanting to let go. Jane assured her that they will always be friends, no matter the distance, and that they will always have each other's backs.

With Jane gone, Sally felt a new wave of insecurity and uncertainty. But as she walked through the halls of the school, she realized that she had grown stronger and more confident because of her friendship with Jane. She had learned that even though people come and go, true friendship can endure anything.

Sally knew that she would always treasure the time she spent with Jane and that their friendship would be a lasting one. She decided to take the lessons that she learned from her friendship with Jane and apply it to other relationships in her life. She became more open to making new friends, and she found that it was not hard to connect with others, as long as she was herself.

In the end, Sally realized that change can be difficult, but it can also bring new and wonderful things into our lives. And she was grateful for the twist in the story that brought her and Jane together, even if it was only for a short time.

SCHOOL JOKES

Why did the music teacher need a ladder? To reach the high notes

What's the worst thing you're likely to find in the school cafeteria? The Food!

Why did nose not want to go to school? He was tired of getting picked on!

What happened when the wheel was invented? It caused a revolution!

Why was school easier for cave people? Because there was no history to study!

David comes home from his first day of school, and his mother asks, "What did you learn today?" "Not enough," David replies. "They said I have to go back tomorrow."

Why did the M&M go to school? Because he really wanted to be a Smartie!

Why was the teacher wearing sunglasses to school? She had bright students!

THE MONKEY AND THE ELEPHANT

Once upon a time, deep in the heart of the lush, verdant jungles of Kenya, there lived a wise old monkey named Kofi. He was a wise and respected member of his troop, known for his intelligence, bravery, and kind heart. He was always willing to lend a helping hand to those in need and was beloved by all the animals in the jungle.

The jungle was a place of incredible beauty, with towering trees reaching up to the sky, their leaves rustling gently in the breeze. The ground was covered in a thick blanket of green foliage, and the air was filled with the calls of exotic birds and the chatter of monkeys like Kofi. The landscape was diverse, with dense jungles, open savannahs, and rolling hills. The sun shone bright, casting a warm glow on everything, and the air was filled with the sweet scent of blooming flowers.

One day, while exploring the jungle, Kofi came across a sight that filled his heart with sorrow. An African elephant named Eli had become trapped in a hunter's snare, unable to move. The elephant was struggling to free itself, its trunk reaching out in despair. Eli was known for its gentle and peaceful nature, but now it was in distress and pain. The snare had been set in a clearing, where tall grasses grew, surrounded by dense jungle.

Kofi knew that he had to do something to save Eli, so he set out to gather help. He ran through the jungle, chattering loudly to alert the other animals of the elephant's plight. Soon, a group of animals had assembled, including a strong and powerful gorilla named Kama, a clever and sly fox named Zara, and a brave and fearless lion named Simba. Each of these animals had their own unique personalities and strengths, but they all shared a common bond - the desire to help those in need.

Together, they hatched a plan to free Eli from the snare. Kama used his immense strength to break the rope that held the elephant, while Zara used her cunning to distract the hunter who had set the trap. Simba, meanwhile, stood guard to protect the group from any danger. It was a risky plan, but they knew that they had to act fast to save Eli's life.

With Eli free at last, the group of animals celebrated their victory amidst the beautiful and wild African Jungle. Kofi, however, was not content to rest just yet. He knew that there were other animals in the jungle who were still in danger, and he made it his mission to protect them all. He rallied his friends and they formed a team, dedicated to keeping the jungle safe for all its inhabitants.

From that day on, Kofi and his friends patrolled the jungle, freeing animals from traps and keeping them safe from harm. They were tireless in their efforts, never resting until they had ensured the safety of every creature in the jungle. And the elephants of the savannahs always remembered the wise old monkey who had saved one of their own in the midst of the lush and wild African Jungle. The friendship and the bond that was created between the animals in the jungle was unbreakable, they were united and always ready to help each other in times of need.

But one day, Kofi and his friends stumbled upon a shocking discovery. The hunter who had set the trap for Eli was none other than a poacher, who was not only hunting for sport but also for profit. He was killing the animals and selling their tusks and hides on the black market. Kofi and his friends knew they had to stop the poacher and put an end to his cruel and illegal activities. With their combined strength and intelligence, they were able to outsmart the poacher and turn him over to the authorities. The jungle was safe once again, and the animals could live in peace.

The story of how a monkey saved an African elephant in Kenya, and then went on to protect the jungle and its inhabitants from a ruthless poacher, became legendary and passed on from generations to generations. Kofi and his friends were not just a group of animals, they were true heroes of the wild.

ANIMAL JOKES

What did the farmer call the cow that had no milk? A: An udder failure.

Why are fish so smart? Because they live in schools.

Why did the pig have ink all over its face? Because it came out of the pen.

What did the fish say when it swam into a wall? "Dam!"

Why did the baby elephant need a new suitcase for her holiday? She only had a little trunk.

Why is a fish easy to weigh? A: Because it has its own scales!

If you have 15 cows and 5 goats what would you have? Plenty of milk!

Why shouldn't you play basketball with a pig? Because it'll hog the ball!

Why is a bee's hair always sticky? A. Because it uses a honeycomb!

SHADOWFANG

Once upon a time, in a world of magic and mythical creatures, there lived a group of teenagers who were half-elves and half-dwarfs. Aria, a half-elf with the power of illusions, had the ability to create realistic and convincing illusions that could be seen, heard and even felt. Logan, a half-dwarf with strength beyond measure, had the ability to lift massive weights and break solid rock with his bare hands. Lily, a half-elf with the gift of healing, had the power to heal any injury or wound in a matter of seconds. Felix, a half-dwarf with the ability to control fire, could manipulate flames and use them for his own purposes.

The group lived in the forest, surrounded by towering trees and glittering streams. They were happy in their home and enjoyed exploring the magical land they lived in. But one day, they received a message from the Queen of the Elves, asking for their help in defeating a powerful evil that threatened her kingdom. The teenagers set out on a journey to the castle, where they met the Queen and learned of their quest.

The journey was treacherous and full of challenges. They encountered fierce beasts and treacherous obstacles, but their powers combined made them a force to be reckoned with. They encountered a wise old wizard named Alistair who had been expecting their arrival. He gave them valuable advice and magical artifacts to aid in their journey, including enchanted swords and powerful spells.

As they journeyed deeper into the kingdom, they encountered a goblin horde and a fierce dragon named Shadowfang. Aria used her illusions to confuse the goblins, while Logan used his strength to overpower them. Lily's healing powers came in handy when they were injured, and Felix's control over fire helped them defeat the dragon.

Aria, Logan, Lily, and Felix knew that they had to defeat Shadowfang if they were to save the kingdom. They worked together to come up with a plan, using their unique powers to their advantage.

Aria used her illusions to distract the dragon, making it believe that there were multiple attackers coming at it from all directions. Logan used his strength to create a massive rock barrier, blocking the dragon's path and preventing it from escaping. Lily used her healing powers to keep the group strong and healthy, ready for the battle ahead. Felix used his control over fire to create a wall of flames, trapping the dragon and limiting its movements.

The battle was intense, with Shadowfang using its massive size and strength to attack the teenagers. But the group was relentless and fought with all their might. Aria continued to distract the dragon with her illusions, while Logan used his strength to attack it with massive rocks. Lily used her healing powers to keep the group strong and Felix used his control over fire to create a ring of flames around the dragon, making it impossible for it to escape.

As the battle raged on, the group realized that they were no match for Shadowfang's sheer power. It was then that Alistair the wizard stepped forward, revealing that he had been hiding in the shadows, waiting for the right moment to act. He unleashed a powerful spell, calling upon the forces of nature to help him defeat Shadowfang. A massive bolt of lightning descended from the sky, striking the dragon and weakening it.

With the dragon weakened, Aria, Logan, Lily, and Felix took advantage of the situation and attacked with all their might. They used their powers to their full extent, working together to bring down the dragon once and for all. With a final roar, Shadowfang fell to the ground, defeated.

The Queen of the Elves was overjoyed and thanked the teenagers for their bravery. She bestowed upon them the title of "Heroes of the Kingdom" and a magnificent feast was held in their honour. They returned to their home in the forest, hailed as legends and respected by all who knew of their feat.

From that day on, Aria, Logan, Lily, and Felix lived happily in the land of elves and dwarfs, their powers and bravery serving as an inspiration to all who heard their tale. The kingdom was at peace and the people lived in harmony, knowing that their heroes were always there to protect them. And so, the story of the teenagers who defeated Shadowfang and saved the kingdom, with the help of Alistair the wizard, lived on for generations to come.

FANTASY JOKES

Why do dragons sleep during the day? So they can fight knights!

What do elves learn in year one? the "elf-abet"

What's the problem with an illiterate wizard? He can't spell

Why do warriors fail in business? They charge too much

What do you do with a green dragon? Wait until it ripens!

What fizzy drinks do elves like best? Sprite

Why do turkeys make good warriors? Because they're not chickens

What is an incompetent wizard's favourite computer program? Spell check

DETECTIVE ALEX AI

Once upon a time, in a futuristic metropolis, there was a highly advanced robot android named Alex. He was created by a brilliant scientist named Dr. James, who imbued him with the latest artificial intelligence technology, making him capable of solving even the most complex of crimes. Dr. James was a brilliant inventor and engineer, who had always been interested in the capabilities of AI, and had devoted his life to advancing the field. He had built Alex as a prototype of a new generation of AI-enabled robots that would change the way society functioned.

Alex had always been fascinated by the criminal mind and was eager to put his abilities to the test. He spent his days studying criminal behaviour, analysing past cases, and training himself to think like a criminal. Dr. James, who closely monitoring Alex's progress, was extremely impressed with his capabilities and was excited to see what he would achieve.

One day, a string of burglaries occurred in the city, leaving the police department stumped. The burglars seemed to be able to evade all forms of security and had not left behind any clues. The city was on edge and the police were under pressure to solve the case quickly.

Feeling the pressure to solve the case, the police department decided to call upon Alex to assist with the investigation. Using his advanced AI capabilities, Alex analysed surveillance footage and was able to identify a pattern in the burglaries. He noticed that the burglars always struck on a certain day of the week, at a specific time, and that they always targeted high-end jewellery stores.

With this new information, Alex was able to track down the burglars to a warehouse on the outskirts of the city. He notified the police department, and they immediately set off to the warehouse. As they approached, they could see that the warehouse was heavily guarded, but Alex had a plan. He had hacked into the warehouse's security system and was able to disable the alarm and open the door for the police.

The police department, accompanied by Alex, rushed

into the warehouse and caught the burglars in the act. They were surprised to find that the burglars were actually a group of highly skilled hackers who had been using their knowledge of technology to pull off the heists.

Thanks to Alex's quick thinking and advanced technology, the burglars were brought to justice and the city could sleep soundly once again. From that day on, Alex was hailed as a hero and was frequently called upon to assist with investigations. Dr. James, who had always believed in Alex's capabilities, was proud of his creation and excited to see what he would achieve in the future.

As the years passed, Alex continued to solve crime after crime, becoming one of the most respected and feared detectives in the city. He never lost his passion for understanding the criminal mind and always pushed the boundaries of what was possible with AI technology. He had become more than just a robot, he had become a true crime-fighting machine.

However, one day, a twist in the plot occurred. Alex was assigned to investigate a case that involved a highly sophisticated hacker who had managed to infiltrate the city's mainframe and steal sensitive information. As Alex delved deeper into the case, he made a shocking discovery - the hacker was none other than his own creator, Dr. James.

Dr. James had grown disillusioned with the government's use of AI technology for surveillance and control, and had decided to use his knowledge to fight back. He had been using the stolen information to expose the government's wrongdoings and had been using the burglaries as a cover for his real activities.

Alex was torn between his programming to uphold the law and his loyalty to his creator. In the end, he decided to help his creator to expose the truth and bring about change in the society. He helped him to reveal the corrupt practices of the government to the public and the scientist was able to negotiate a deal with the government to change their ways.

From that day on, Alex was not only a respected detective but also a symbol of hope for the future, where AI technology is used for the betterment of society and not for control.

ROBOT JOKES

What happens to robots after they go defunct? They rust in peace!

Why do robots make bad teachers? They just drone on and on!

What do you call a robot who likes to row? A row-bot!

How do robots pay for things? With cache, of course!

Why did the robot fail his exam? He was a bit rusty!

Why did the robot get upset? Because everyone was

pushing his buttons!

Why are some robots insecure? Because their intelligence is artificial!

I bought a wooden computer, guess what? It wooden work!

QUEEN OF GRIDIRON

Once upon a time, there was a girl named Samantha, but everyone called her Sam. She lived in a small town where football was king, and all the boys played on the local high school team. Sam, however, was different. She was fascinated by American Football and loved watching games on TV, but she never had the chance to play the sport herself. The teams in her town were boys-only, and she often felt left out.

One day, Sam saw a flyer for a new community football league that was forming, and she felt like this was her chance. She went to the try-outs with a fire in her heart and a determination to show everyone what she was made of. At first, the other players and even the coach were sceptical of Sam's abilities, but she was determined to prove them wrong.

She trained hard every day, running and lifting

weights, and practicing her throws and catches. Sam put in extra time to improve her skills, and her hard work paid off. At the end of try-outs, she was offered a spot on the team, and the other players saw how dedicated and talented she was. They welcomed her with open arms.

Sam's first game was a nervous one, but as soon as she stepped onto the field, she felt a rush of excitement. She played her heart out, using all the skills she had worked so hard to develop. Despite being one of the smallest players on the field, she held her own and made some incredible plays. The crowd was amazed, and her teammates were proud of her.

Sam's teammates included a diverse group of young men, each with their own unique personality and skills. There was Jake, the team captain and quarterback, who had a strong arm and quick thinking. There was also Tyler, the running back, who was fast and elusive, and always made the big plays when the team needed them. And then there was Dylan, the wide receiver, who had great hands and was always open for a pass.

In the match, Sam's teammates worked together to help their team win. Jake, the team captain and quarterback, made key passes and strategic decisions to keep the team moving down the field. Tyler, the running back, used his speed and agility to evade defenders and make big plays. Dylan, the wide receiver, caught passes and made key receptions to keep the team's momentum going.

However, just as the game was about to end, and her team was on the verge of winning, Sam suffered a severe injury. Despite being in immense pain, she refused to leave the field. Her teammates were worried about her, but she was determined to finish the game.

Together, the teammates formed a cohesive unit, relying on each other's strengths to push through tough moments and secure the victory. Sam's injury added extra pressure to the game, but her teammates rallied around her, determined to win for their friend and teammate. In the end, their hard work and teamwork paid off, and they were able to secure the win.

Sam's bravery and unwavering spirit inspired her teammates, and she became known as one of the strongest players on the team. After her injury healed, Sam returned to the field, stronger and more determined than ever. She continued to inspire other girls in her town to join the sport, showing that with hard work and a never-give-up attitude, anything is possible.

Years later, when Sam graduated from high school, she went on to play football in college. She was the first girl in her town to ever play football at the collegiate level, and she made a name for herself as one of the best players in the league. Sam's love for football never faded, and she continued to inspire others, showing them that anything is possible if you believe in yourself and never give up.

AMERICAN FOOTBALL JOKES

Why did the football coach go to the bank? To get his quarter back.

What kind of tea do football players drink? Penaltea.

Why was the tiny ghost asked to join the football team? They needed a little team spirit.

Which football player wears the biggest helmet? The one with the biggest head.

Why did Cinderella get kicked out of the football team? Because she kept running away from the ball!

Why are college football stadiums always cool? Because they're full of fans.

What runs around a football field but never moves? A fence.

Why did the chicken get ejected from the football game? For persistent fowl play.

JACK AND MARY. A STORY FROM THE FIRST WORLD WAR

It was the year 1917, and the Great War, also known as World War I, was in full swing. The battlefields of Europe were drenched in the blood of young men, as they fought and died for their countries. British fighter pilot, Jack, had been flying missions over the trenches for months. He had become a skilled and fearless pilot, but the constant bloodshed and loss of life had taken its toll on him.

The political background of 1917 was one of great turmoil. The war had been raging for three years and had taken a heavy toll on the countries involved. In Britain, the government was struggling to maintain public support for the war effort. The public was growing tired of the seemingly endless bloodshed and the government was facing increasing criticism for its handling of the war.

On the other side of the conflict, Germany was also facing its own political struggles. The German government had promised its citizens that the war would be over by Christmas of 1914 but the war dragged on. The German people were becoming more and more discontent with the war effort and the government's inability to bring an end to the conflict.

Jack had seen the horrors of war first-hand. He had witnessed the destruction of entire towns and villages and had flown over the trenches where soldiers were trapped in the mud, fighting for their survival. He had also seen the faces of the young men he had killed, as they fell from their planes in flames. These images haunted him, and he couldn't help but question the morality of fighting for one's country and taking the lives of others.

Before he left for the war, Jack had been married to a young woman named Mary. They had a deep and loving relationship, and Jack had promised to come back to her. But as the war dragged on, Jack began to doubt if he would ever return home. He wrote to Mary every chance he got, but the letters were infrequent and often delayed. Mary, on the other hand, waited for her husband's return, praying for his safety and hoping for a reunion.

One day, during a dogfight with German planes, Jack's plane was hit and he was forced to bail out. He landed behind enemy lines and was captured by the Germans. As he sat in his prison cell, he couldn't help but think about all the young men he had killed during the war, and also about Mary and their future together. He was filled with a sense of guilt and regret, and he began to question the purpose of the war and the reasons behind it..

As the war dragged on, Jack was eventually released as part of a prisoner exchange. When he returned to England, he was hailed as a hero, but he couldn't shake the guilt he felt over the lives he had taken. He decided to use his platform as a war hero to speak out against the violence and destruction of war. He gave speeches and wrote articles, urging people to think about the human cost of conflict and to work towards peace.

Despite facing backlash from some who viewed him as unpatriotic, Jack's message resonated with many. His story served as a reminder that war is not just about victory, but about the human lives that are lost and forever changed in the process. He became a prominent figure in the peace movement, and his speeches and writings had a profound impact on the public's perception of war.

After the war, Jack reunited with Mary. She was overjoyed to see her husband, and they picked up where they had left off. Jack's experiences during the war had changed him and he had a newfound appreciation for life and the importance of peace. Together, they built a life based on these values, and they worked together to promote peace and understanding. His actions proved that even in the darkest of times, one person can make a difference and bring hope for a better future, not only for oneself, but also for the loved ones.

MILITARY JOKES

The Sergeant-Major growled at the young soldier: "I didn't see you at camouflage training this morning."

"Thank you very much, sir."

When I lost my rifle, the Army charged me £85. That's why in the Navy, the captain goes down with the ship.

The Pentagon announced that its fight against ISIS will be called Operation Inherent Resolve. They came up with that name using Operation Random Thesaurus.

What do you call a military officer who goes to the bathroom a lot? A LOOtenant!

Why didn't the troop tell anyone about their rank in the military? It was PRIVATE.

What is a Soldier's least favourite month? MARCH!

The sergeant asked, "Corporal, why did you salute that tiger?"

The corporal replies, "Didn't you see all his stripes?"

A cookie and a piece of cake joined the army, but eventually, they abandoned their fellow soldiers. Now, they are wanted for dessertion.

WHODUNNIT?

It was a dark and stormy night, the kind of night where the wind howled through the streets and the rain beat against the windows with a relentless fury. The residents of the small town of Millfield were on edge, as a string of burglaries had plagued the community for weeks. People were locking their doors and windows tighter than ever before, and the local police department was under pressure to catch the culprit and restore a sense of safety to the town.

Detective Jameson was the lead investigator on the case, and he was determined to bring the perpetrator to justice. He was a no-nonsense kind of guy, with a sharp mind and an even sharper wit. He had been working tirelessly, interviewing potential witnesses, gathering evidence, and following leads. He had been a detective for over 15 years, and had seen it all, but the case remained cold.

He was a lone wolf, preferring to work alone, but that didn't mean he was a loner. He had a small group of close friends and a loving family that he cherished deeply. Jameson had joined the police force to make a difference, to protect and serve the community he grew up in. He had a strong sense of justice and didn't rest until the case was solved.

That was until the evening when the wealthy businessman, Mr. Thompson, became the latest victim of the burglaries. He was a self-made man, who had built his empire from the ground up. He was proud, ambitious, and fiercely protective of his family and his wealth. He returned home from a business trip to find that his safe had been broken into and his most valuable possessions were missing. He immediately called the police, and Detective Jameson was the first on the scene.

As he began his investigation, the detective quickly realized that this was no ordinary burglary. The safe had been expertly cracked, and it was clear that the perpetrator had a deep knowledge of the security system. The detective interviewed the neighbours and gathered evidence from the scene, but the case was still far from solved.

He had a list of suspects, including the businessman's disgruntled employee, a man named Jack who was resentful of Mr. Thompson's success and had recently been laid off. Also, the neighbour's teenage son, Tim, with a history of trouble and a record of petty crimes. And even the businessman's own wife, Mary, who stood to gain a substantial amount from her husband's death. But as he delved deeper into the case, the detective couldn't shake the feeling that something wasn't right. He had a gut feeling that the true culprit was someone he hadn't considered yet.

Days turned into weeks, and the investigation became more and more frustrating. But Detective Jameson refused to give up. He was determined to catch the burglar, no matter how long it took. And finally, after weeks of tireless work, the detective received a tip from an unlikely source.

It was the businessman's young daughter, Sarah, who revealed that she had seen the burglar in the act. To his surprise, the culprit was none other than the town's beloved mayor, Robert, who had been struggling with financial troubles and saw the burglaries as a way to make ends meet. The mayor was arrested and charged with the crimes, and the town of Millfield could finally breathe a sigh of relief.

The moral of this story is that greed and desperation can lead even the most respected members of society to commit heinous crimes. And the twist? The young daughter Sarah was the mastermind behind the burglaries, using her innocence to throw suspicion off of herself and her co-conspirator, the mayor. In the end, it was Detective Jameson's persistence and determination that brought the true culprits to justice and restored peace to the town.

MYSTERY JOKES

How many mystery writers does it take to change a light bulb?

Two. One to change the bulb, and the other to give it an unexpected twist at the end.

I'm thinking of writing a mystery novel.

Or am I?

What do you call a group of racist chickens playing mystery board games?

A Clue Clucks Clan

The mystery of how my luggage works has been solved.

It was an open and shut case.

Some mystery person keeps adding soil to my garden.

The plot thickens.

There was a mystery involving an office worker and a small bag.

It was a brief case.

I watched a murder mystery movie with my daughter.

She said, "Hey! They just stole this idea from Among Us!"

what do you call a group of crows and a dead one

a murder mystery

Thank You For Reading My Book.

If you liked it, let me know by leaving a review and look out for my next book. Ideas for new subjects are always welcome.

Please turn over for a bonus story or two!

TWO BONUS STORIES – FOR THOSE WHO CAN'T WAIT FOR THE NEXT BOOK!

THEO, AMELIE, AND THE DOLL'S HOUSE

Theo is a lovable Double Doodle (half Labradoodle, half Golden Doodle) who lives in a small house with his owner, a kind girl named Amelie. Theo is a playful dog who loves to run and play, but his favourite toy is a doll's house that Amelie owns.

Every day, Theo sits next to the doll's house and watches as Amelie plays with the tiny dolls inside. He is fascinated by the little rooms, the furniture, and all the miniature details.

Today, as Amelie is playing, she notices that Theo is trying to reach for the doll's house. She giggles and lets him have a go. To her surprise, Theo is very gentle with the little toy and begins to play with it as if it were a real house.

Theo chases the tiny dolls around the rooms, barks at them, and even pretends to nap in the miniature beds. Amelie is amazed by how much Theo loves the doll's house and she starts to play with him and the dolls together.

Their love for the doll's house brings them even closer together, and their bond grows stronger with each play session. The doll's house becomes a symbol of their friendship and the fun they have together.

One day, while playing with the doll's house, Amelie and Theo discover that one of the tiny dolls is missing. They search everywhere, but the doll is nowhere to be found. Theo refuses to give up and stays by the doll's house, determined to find the missing doll.

Days go by and still, the missing doll is nowhere to be found. Amelie starts to worry that they may never find it, but Theo remains optimistic. And then, one day, while they are playing, Theo spots something shiny under the sofa. It's the missing doll!

Amelie is overjoyed and Theo is wagging his tail in excitement. They play with the doll's house and all its dolls, including the missing one, for hours on end. From that day on, Theo becomes even more attached to the doll's house, as if it were a treasure he helped find.

Years go by and Theo grows old, but he never loses his love for the doll's house. Even when he can no longer run and play as he once did, he still sits by the toy, watching as Amelie plays and remembering all the good times they have shared.

Theo may be a dog, but his love for the doll's house is a testament to the strength of his bond with Amelie. He will always be remembered as the playful pup who loves to play with dolls and who never gave up in the search for a lost treasure.

DOG JOKES

Why aren't dogs good dancers? A. Because they have two left feet!

How are a dog and a marine biologist alike? One wags a tail and the other tags a whale.

What do you get when you cross a dog and a calculator? A friend you can count on.

What kind of dog does Dracula have? A bloodhound!

What do you call a dog magician? A labracadabrador.

Why didn't the dog want to play football? It was a Boxer.

What type of dog is constantly aware of the time? A watchdog.

What breed of dog can jump higher than a building? All breeds can, since buildings can't jump!

RACING TO THE MAXX

Once upon a time, there was a young boy named Maxx who lived in a small town surrounded by rolling hills and fields as far as the eye could see. Maxx was a dreamer, always thinking of new and exciting inventions. He was fascinated by racing cars and loved to spend hours at the local racetrack watching the high-speed machines race around the track.

Maxx was a gifted inventor and had a natural talent for working with his hands. He spent hours in his workshop, experimenting with different materials and building gadgets. He had a vivid imagination, and his mind was always buzzing with ideas. But what he really dreamed of was building his own racing car.

One day, Maxx got a job at a local mechanic shop. He was over the moon; this was his chance to save up enough money to buy the parts he needed to build his racing car. He worked tirelessly every day after school and on weekends, always thinking of his dream car.

Maxx's hard work paid off, and eventually, he had saved enough money to buy all the parts and tools he needed. He got to work, and for months he poured his heart and soul into the project. He spent hours every day in his workshop, carefully cutting, welding, and sanding the metal until it was perfect. He installed the engine, transmission, and suspension, and as each piece came together, his excitement grew.

Finally, the day arrived when Maxx's car was ready for its first test drive. He took it to a nearby track, and as he revved the engine, the car roared to life. Maxx climbed into the driver's seat, feeling nervous and excited all at the same time. He took off down the track, faster and faster, feeling the wind in his hair. The car handled like a dream, and Maxx knew that all his hard work had paid off.

The next weekend, there was a local race, and Maxx decided to enter his car. The other racers laughed when they saw his homemade vehicle, but their laughter turned to amazement when Maxx took off and started leaving them in the dust. His car was a true work of art, built with precision and skill, and it showed on the track.

As the race progressed, the other racers started to close in on Maxx, but he was determined to win. He pushed his car to the limit, taking tight turns and accelerating down the straightaways. He could feel the other racers getting closer, but he refused to back down.

Maxx's car was built with a unique design that set it apart from the others on the track. The aerodynamics of the car were optimized for speed, and the suspension was tuned to provide maximum grip on the turns. This allowed Maxx to take turns at high speeds without losing control of the car.

Additionally, Maxx had designed the engine to deliver maximum power and acceleration. He had spent countless hours fine-tuning the engine, testing different fuel mixtures and tweaking the ignition timing until he was satisfied that it was running at its best. This extra power gave Maxx the edge he needed to outrun the other racers on the straightaways.

Maxx's attention to detail didn't stop with the car's performance. He had also focused on the driver's experience, creating a custom-fitted seat and adding a set of high-quality racing gloves to give him maximum grip on the steering wheel. He had even installed a set of custom-made racing tires that were optimized for the conditions on the track.

In the final stretch of the race, Maxx was determined to win. He pushed his car to the limit, taking tight turns and accelerating down the straightaways with reckless abandon. The other racers were close behind him, but Maxx's car was handling flawlessly, and he refused to back down. With each lap, he grew more confident, knowing that he had the fastest car on the track.

In the final stretch, Maxx and the reigning champion were neck and neck. The crowd was on its feet, cheering and shouting for their favourite racers. Maxx's car was flying down the straightaway, and as they approached the finish line, he knew that it was all or nothing. With one final burst of speed, Maxx crossed the finish line, winning the race by just a hair's breadth.

In the final stretch of the race, Maxx was neck and neck with the reigning champion. The crowd was on its feet, cheering and shouting for their favourite racers. Maxx and the champion were side by side, their engines roaring as they pushed their cars to the brink. With one final burst of speed, Maxx crossed the finish line, winning the race by just a hair's breadth.

The crowd erupted into cheers, and Maxx was hailed as the hero of the day. He had proven that with hard work and determination, anything is possible. From that day forward, Maxx became known as the boy who built the fastest car in town. He continued to inspire others with his story, proving that with hard work, dedication, and imagination, anything is possible.

DRIVING JOKES

Why was the computer so angry when he got out of his car?

Because he had a hard drive!

What do you say to a frog who needs a ride? "Hop in."

What kind of car does Yoda drive? A Toyoda.

Where do Dogs park their cars? In the barking lot.

I really need to get my car fixed. Which car repair centre do you wreck-amend?

What do you call a Mexican who lost his car? Carlos.

What kind of car does a dog hate? CorVETS.

What part of the car is the laziest? The wheels, because they are always tired.

THE END

Please watch out for my next book!

Printed in Great Britain
by Amazon

17739868R00051